Terry's Tru
The Wartime
Watch

by Mick Gowar

"Dad?"

No answer.

"Daad?"

Terry's dad sighed and looked up from the reception desk where he was busy with an untidy pile of papers.

"Yes, Terry – what is it now?"

"Were you alive in the war, Dad?"

Dad frowned. "It depends which war you mean. I was alive during the Falklands War and the Gulf War, of course. Why?"

"It's for school. Everyone's got to bring in something from the Second World War and give a talk about it."

"I wasn't born then," said Dad. "When do you have to give this talk?"

"Er, tomorrow …"

Dad groaned. "Why do you always have to leave things 'til the last minute? I'm sorry. I've got all these bills to sort out. I'd like to help you, but …" He pointed to the huge pile of paper.

"Is there anything I can take in to school?" asked Terry. "Is there anything in the hotel that's really old?"

"Only the plumbing," replied Dad. "Go and ask your mum. I'm far too busy. And next time, get yourself organised!"

Terry looked in the lounge, the dining room and the kitchen – no Mum. He plodded upstairs towards the family's small flat on the second floor. Things looked bad. He was going to be in big trouble.

As he got to the second floor landing, Terry noticed
that the small door leading to the attic was open.
Mum must be up there, he thought. As he reached
the top of the narrow stairs he heard sounds
coming from the first attic room. Terry looked
round the half-open door. Mum was on her hands
and knees peering at the skirting board.

"Mum?"

"I'm busy, can't it wait?"

"What are you doing?"

"Looking for holes. One of the guests said she saw a mouse, so I'm checking." She stood up. "What is it, Terry – but be quick."

"Do you know anything about the war – the Second World War, I mean?"

"Not really," said Mum. "Just that Grandpa came down here as an evacuee. That's how he met Grandma – at the local school, the same one you go to."

"What's an evacuee?" asked Terry.

"That's what they called children from London and the other big cities, who were sent to live in the country, or by the sea, so they'd be safe from the bombing."

"Bombing …?"

"Yes," said Mum. "During the war the Germans bombed the big cities. Hundreds of planes every night would bomb London, Liverpool and the other cities."

"Why did the Germans bomb London and Liverpool?"

"You don't know much, do you Terry? The Germans were the enemy in those days. Anyway, why are you asking me all this?"

"It's for school. We've got to bring something in and talk about it, and it's got to be something to do with the war. And it's for tomorrow."

"Oh, Terry," sighed Mum, heading for the door. "Why do you always leave it 'til the last moment?"

Terry suddenly had a brilliant idea.

"I'll phone Grandpa, and ask him all about being an evacuee!"

"You'll be lucky," said Mum. "Grandpa and Grandma have gone to Spain for a week, remember? I've got mice to find. You'll just have to sort it out yourself."

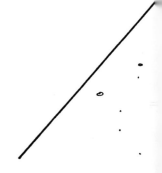

13

Terry was alone in the room – apart from the old-fashioned wardrobe. In the wardrobe, Terry knew, was the old lost-property trunk. It was full of old things, but every time Terry took something out of the trunk strange things happened.

Terry thought for a moment. Dare he risk opening the trunk again? Yes – this was an emergency. He opened the wardrobe door and threw back the lid of the trunk. It was just as he'd first found it – except for the magician's hat and the strong man's leopard-skin shorts which had caused so many problems. He peered into the trunk. There had to be something old and harmless he could take to school.

He rummaged around in the trunk until his hand closed around something cold and round. It was an old-fashioned gold watch. On the back was engraved:

Time marches on
But these days will live
When we have all gone
June, 1940

1940! That was during the war! It was perfect!

"I don't suppose it still works," thought Terry. He turned the little gold knob on the side. Immediately the watch began to tick. Terry glanced at his own watch: 5.30.

He started to turn the hands back to the correct time when the room began to spin. Everything seemed to whirl and blur, like a fairground roundabout but much, much faster.

"'Ello," said a voice. "Where d'you come from?"

"Uhhh?" Terry opened his eyes. He was sitting on a grassy bank with his back against a tall hedge. In front of him was a dusty country lane. Sitting next to him was a boy of about his age, but dressed in strange clothes. He was wearing a pair of knee-length grey shorts, a grey jacket, and he had a red and yellow striped cap perched on the back of his head.

"I ain't seen you round here before," said the boy. "Are you an evacuee or something?"

"Er – yes, I suppose so," said Terry.

"Me too," said the boy. "I'm from Whitechapel – that's in London. I was sent down 'ere to get out of the Blitz. But I wish I was back there."

The boy looked suspiciously at Terry. "You foreign or something? You ain't 'alf got funny clothes."

"Er – no," said Terry.

"Only you can't be too careful these days." The boy's voice dropped to a whisper. "They say there's German spies everywhere."

There was something very familiar about the boy. Terry was sure he'd seen him before somewhere.

"'Ere – you got any chocolate?" asked the boy. "I've used up all me sweet ration. No more sweets 'til next month."

Terry felt in his pockets. "I've got this …" He held out a packet of bubble gum.

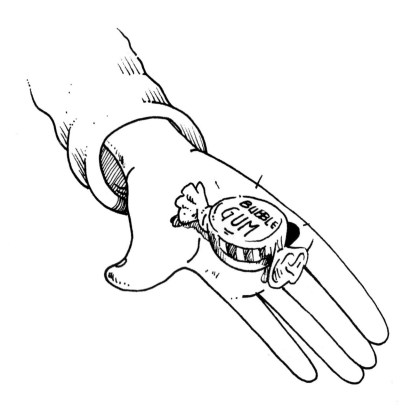

"Crikey!" said the boy. "Just like the yanks have. But I've never seen that sort before. I'll swap you ..."

And he pulled a tiny silver aeroplane out of his jacket pocket.

"It's a Spitfire," he said proudly.

"What's a ..."

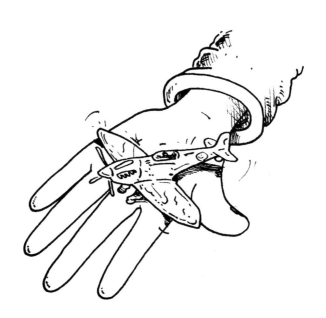

But before Terry could finish his question there was a deafening roar. Two planes suddenly appeared overhead, just skimming the treetops.

"It's a dog-fight!" yelled the boy. "Come on, let's go and watch."

He ran a short way along the lane to a gate leading to a sloping grassy field.

"Come on!" shouted the boy. "We don't want to miss it!"

They ran up the slope as one of the planes started to climb, higher and higher into the clear, blue sky. The second plane followed, just a few metres behind.

"It's a Messerschmidt!" yelled the boy, excitedly pointing to the plane in front. Terry could just see black crosses painted on the undersides of the wings.

"And the one behind?" asked Terry.

"Blimey! Don't you know nothing?" said the other boy. "That's a Spitfire – like the one you've just got. Look!"

Two bursts of what looked like sparks came from the front edge of the Spitfire's wing. A second later the rattle of machine-gun fire reached the boys. Smoke began to stream from the Messerschmidt's tail.

"That'll teach you!" screamed the boy, shaking his fist at the German plane. It levelled off for a moment before falling into a steep dive. Terry waited for the pilot to pull it up, but down it fell – faster and faster and faster. It smashed into a small clump of trees a few hundred metres from where the boys were standing.

"He's bailed out!" yelled the boy, pointing to a fluffy blob slowly floating towards the ground.

The two boys gazed up as the parachute floated down into the field. The pilot hit the ground with a thump just a few metres from where the boys were standing. The parachute floated down over him.

Slowly a figure crawled out from under the parachute. It was a young man of about 20 years old. He was dressed in a grey uniform and had a leather helmet on his head. He lay still on the ground, beside his parachute, groaning. Terry could see that his right leg was twisted. It was obviously broken.

"Strewth!" said the boy. "What do we do now?"

"Shouldn't we help him?" suggested Terry.

"But he's a German!" said the boy.

Before they could do anything a loud voice bellowed across the field: "Stand back, you boys. He may be armed!"

A fat policemen was hurrying up the slope. He was pushing an old-fashioned bicycle. He dropped the bike and drew a long wooden truncheon from his pocket.

"Right you," he boomed at the young airman. "You are under arrest – understand?"

The young airman raised his head, nodded, and then fainted.

"You two boys had best go home," said the policeman. "But I'll have to take your names later. For the official report. Speaking of which – would either of you happen to know the time. My watch seems to have – erm – stopped."

Terry looked at his wristwatch: 5.30. That couldn't
be right. He reached into his pocket for the old gold
watch. But as he grasped it, the field, the trees, the
boy, the policeman and the airman – everything
began to spin faster and faster.

Terry closed his eyes until the spinning stopped.
When he opened them again, he was back in the
attic room.

Terry looked at his watch: 5.30. It was working, but no time had passed. That was impossible. He reached into his jeans pocket for the gold watch. It wasn't there, but something else was. Terry pulled it out. It was the little silver plane.

Terry stared at the little plane. He didn't have the watch anymore, but he did have something even better to take to school tomorrow. He also had a story to tell about the war. Maybe no one would believe him, but Terry knew it was true.

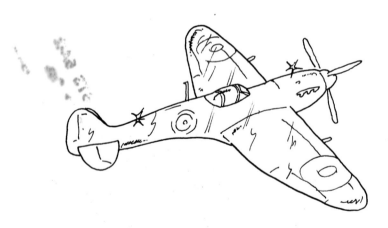